My First Golden Dictionary

Compiled by
Tina Thoburn

Illustrated by
Jean Chandler

A GOLDEN BOOK · NEW YORK
Western Publishing Company, Inc., Racine, Wisconsin 53404

A a

airplane An **airplane** flies high in the sky.

alphabet There are 26 letters in the **alphabet.** We use the letters to make words.

Aa Bb Cc Dd Ee
Ff Gg Hh Ii Jj Kk
Ll Mm Nn Oo Pp
Qq Rr Ss Tt Uu
Vv Ww Xx Yy Zz

aquarium An **aquarium** is a home for fish and snails.

astronaut An **astronaut** flies through space in a spacecraft.

B b

baby A **baby** is a tiny new person.

ball My **ball** is round. It bounces high.

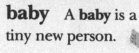

balloon My **balloon** is round, like a ball. It floats in the air.

barn A **barn** is a big house for farm animals.

bath I take a **bath** in a bathtub.

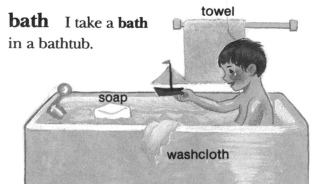

towel

soap

washcloth

beach A **beach** is a sandy place beside the water.

birthday My **birthday** is the day I was born. At my **birthday** party I blow out the candles on my cake.

beads **Beads** have little holes. I string **beads** to wear around my neck.

boat We use a **boat** to travel on water.

bed I sleep in my **bed**. I cover up with a blanket.

blanket

pillow

body My **body** is all of me. My **body** has many parts.

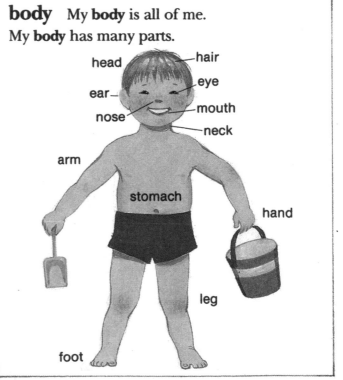

head

hair

ear

eye

nose

mouth

neck

arm

stomach

hand

leg

foot

bicycle I ride my **bicycle**. It has two big wheels.

bird A **bird** is covered with feathers. Most **birds** can fly.

book A **book** has words and sometimes pictures. Grandpa is reading a **book** to me.

bottle   A **bottle** holds liquid, such as milk or juice.

box   A **box** holds things. I put my toys in a **box.**

boy   My brother is a **boy.** My father was a **boy** before he grew up.

brush   A **brush** has bristles. We use some **brushes** for cleaning, some for painting, and some for our hair.

bubbles   I blow **bubbles** in the air. They go pop!

Cc

camera   We take photographs with a **camera.**

can   A **can** is made of metal. It keeps food safe to eat.

car   A **car** has four wheels and a motor. We ride in it.

cat   A **cat** is a grown-up kitten. My **cat** says "Meow."

chair   My **chair** has a seat, a back, and four legs. Grandma has a rocking **chair.**

climb I **climb** the ladder. I go up and up.

clock A **clock** tells the time. School starts at nine o'clock.

clothes I wear **clothes** to cover my body and keep warm.

T-shirt

dress

sweater

jeans

shorts

jacket

clown The **clown** does funny tricks to make us laugh.

colors Crayons are different **colors.**

black

orange

yellow

purple

brown

green

blue

red

cookie A **cookie** is a small flat cake. **Cookies** and milk are good for dessert.

cow We get milk from a **cow.** A baby **cow** is a calf.

Dd

dance To **dance** I move my feet and body to music.

dish A **dish** holds food. I set the **dishes** on the table.

bowl
plate
cup
saucer

doctor A **doctor** helps sick people get well. **Doctors** often work in hospitals.

dog A **dog** is a grown-up puppy. My **dog** barks and wags his tail.

drum My **drum** makes a loud sound when I bang on it.

duck A **duck** has webbed feet. **Ducks** can swim.

Ee

eat When I eat, I put food in my mouth, chew it, and swallow it.

fork
spoon
knife
sandwich

elephant An **elephant** has big ears and a long trunk.

exercise I **exercise** to keep my body strong.

Ff

farmer A **farmer** grows food for us to eat. A **farmer** raises animals, too.

fire fighter A **fire fighter** puts out fires. **Fire fighters** use fire trucks to get to the fires.

firehouse

hose

ladder

fire truck

fire fighter

fish A **fish** lives in water. Its body is covered with scales.

flag The **flag** of the United States is red, white, and blue. It has stars and stripes.

flashlight I turn on my **flashlight** so its beam of light can help me see in the dark.

flower A **flower** grows on a plant. I pick pretty **flowers** for my friend.

fly To **fly** is to move through the air above the ground.

frog A **frog** can live near or in a pond. **Frogs** leap from place to place.

fruit **Fruit** is good to eat. I eat **fruit** for dessert or as a snack.

grapes

cherry

apple

banana

peach

strawberry

pear

pineapple

orange

watermelon

933339

Gg

garden We grow flowers and vegetables in our **garden.**

rake

shovel

hoe

girl My sister is a **girl.** My mother was a **girl** before she grew up.

glasses **Glasses** help people see better. Sunglasses shade their eyes from the sun.

goat Some **goats** have horns. A baby **goat** is a kid.

guitar A **guitar** makes music when I pluck the strings. I like to play my **guitar** and sing.

Hh

brush

barrette

hair **Hair** grows on top of my head. I use a brush or a comb to keep it neat.

comb

hat I wear a **hat** on my head.

helicopter A **helicopter** flies when its rotors go around.

help To **help** I do something for someone or with someone.

hen   A **hen** lays eggs. Some of them hatch into baby chicks.

horse   A **horse** is fun to ride. A baby **horse** is a foal.

house   A **house** is a place where people live.

chimney

roof

window

door

hug   To **hug** we put our arms around each other.

Ii

ice   **Ice** is frozen water.

ice cream   **Ice cream** is cold and tastes sweet.

insects   **Insects** are bugs. They have six legs.

ant

bee

butterfly

grasshopper

mosquito

beetle

fly

ladybug

Jj

jack-o'-lantern A **jack-o'-lantern** is a pumpkin with a face.

jelly   **Jelly** is good to eat with peanut butter on bread.

juice I squeeze fruit to get **juice.** I like to drink a glass of **juice.**

jump To **jump** I leap in the air. I like to **jump** rope.

Kk

kangaroo A **kangaroo** hops. A baby **kangaroo** rides in its mother's pouch.

key A **key** opens a lock, starts a car, or winds a clock.

kick I **kick** a soccer ball with my foot.

kitchen A **kitchen** is a room where we prepare food.

refrigerator

cupboard

sink

counter

stove

kite My **kite** flies high in the wind.

Ll

lamb A **lamb** is a baby sheep. It has soft, curly wool.

lamp A **lamp** gives light so I can see at night.

laugh We **laugh** when something is funny.

laundry We wash, dry, and iron clothes in the **laundry.**

basket

washer   dryer

hangers

iron

ironing board

letter I write a **letter** to my friend. I put a stamp on the envelope.

Dear Kim,

library There are many books in a **library.** The librarian helps me choose a book to borrow.

living room After dinner we sit in the **living room.**

curtains

chair

stairs

rug

piano

TV

sofa

Mm

magnet A **magnet** can pick up things made of iron and steel.

magnifying glass A **magnifying glass** makes things look bigger than they are.

mail carrier A **mail carrier** delivers letters and packages.

man A **man** is a grown-up boy. My daddy is a **man.**

merry-go-round We ride around and around on a **merry-go-round.**

mirror I can see myself in a **mirror.**

money We spend **money** to buy things.

penny

nickel

dime

dollar

moon The **moon** gives us light at night.

mouse A **mouse** is small and furry. It has a long tail.

Nn

nest A **nest** is a home for birds.

numbers We use **numbers** to count things.

one
1

two
2

three
3

four
4

five
5

six
6

seven
7

eight
8

nine
9

ten
10

nurse A **nurse** helps a doctor. **Nurses** often work in hospitals.

nut   A **nut** has a hard shell. The inside is usually good to eat.

Pp

paint   I **paint** a picture with my **paints.**

Oo

hot   cold

opposites   **Opposites** are two words with very different meanings.

little

soft

hard

big

new   old

happy   sad

pan   I use a **pan** to cook and bake. I also cook in a pot.

pans

pots

parade   In a **parade** many people march together. A band plays. The crowd cheers.

orchestra   People in an **orchestra** make music together by playing instruments.

pencil   I write with a **pencil.** Sometimes I erase.

A B C

owl   An **owl** is a bird with big eyes. It flies at night.

picture   I drew a **picture** of my puppy. I will hang it on the wall.

pig A **pig** is a farm animal with a curly tail. A baby pig is a piglet.

pizza **Pizza** is good to eat. It is made of dough, tomato sauce, and cheese.

playground A **playground** is a place to play.

slide

swings

sandbox

seesaw

jungle gym

police officer A **police officer** protects and helps people.

popcorn **Popcorn** pops when it is cooked. **Popcorn** is fun to eat.

puppet I put a **puppet** on my hand. It moves when I wiggle my fingers.

Qq

quilt I sleep under a warm **quilt.** It is made from pieces of cloth.

Rr

rabbit A **rabbit** has long ears and a short tail.

radio I listen to music and talk shows on the **radio.**

rainbow I saw a **rainbow** in the sky. It was raining and the sun was shining.

record When I play my **record** on a record player, I hear music.

ring A **ring** is round. I wear **rings** on my fingers.

robot A **robot** is a machine. It does jobs people can do.

run To **run** we move our feet fast. We race to see who **runs** the fastest.

Ss

blackboard

school In **school** we learn to read and write.

desk

scissors I use **scissors** to cut paper and string.

seashell A **seashell** is a home for a sea creature. We find **seashells** on the beach.

shapes I draw many **shapes** on my paper.

circle

rectangle

square

diamond

triangle

oval

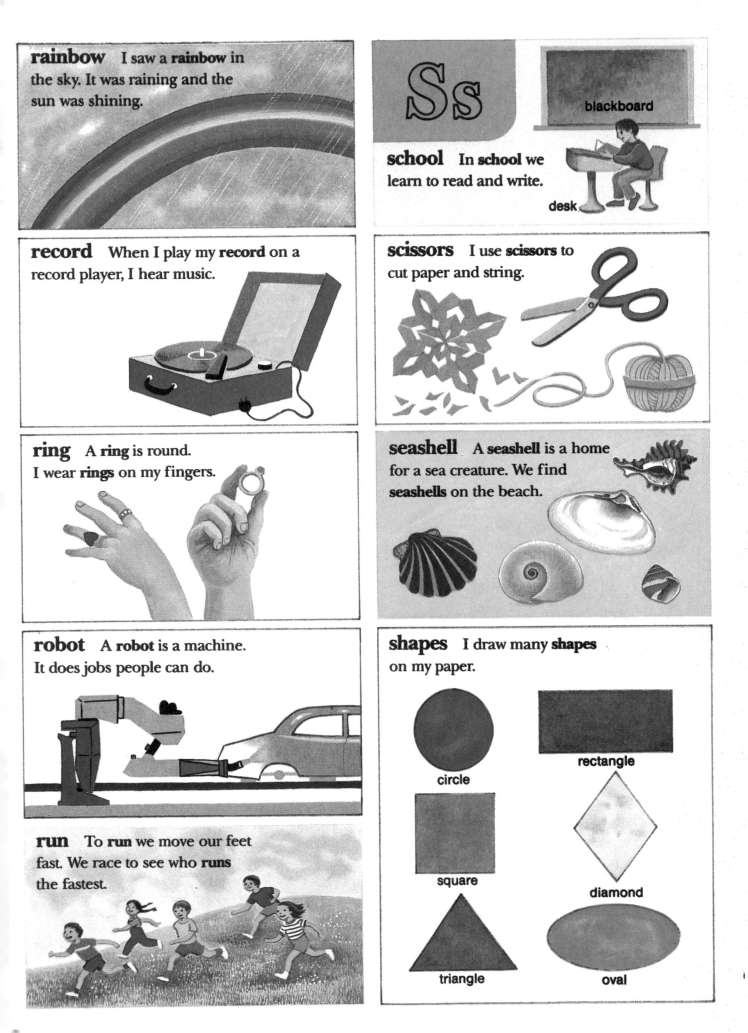

shoes We wear **shoes** on our feet.

socks **Socks** come in pairs. We wear them on our feet inside our shoes.

skates My roller **skates** roll on wheels. My ice **skates** glide on runners.

squirrel A **squirrel** has a bushy tail. It scampers up a tree.

sleep I **sleep** to rest my body. I close my eyes when I **sleep.**

night-light

star **Stars** twinkle in the sky. They are very far away.

snow **Snow** is cold and fluffy. We do many things in the **snow.**

snowman

snowflake

skis

sled

snow shovel

snowmobile

store We buy things in a **store.** At the shopping mall there are many **stores.**

OYS PETS BOOKS SHOES SUPERMARKET

street Cars and trucks ride on the **street.** We cross the **street** at the corner.

traffic light

corner

sidewalk

suitcase I pack my things in a **suitcase** to go on a trip.

sun The **sun** shines in the daytime. It makes me feel warm.

swim To **swim** through water I move my arms and legs.

table A **table** has legs and a flat top. I eat at a **table.**

teacher A **teacher** helps children learn. I like my **teacher.**

$2 \times 1 = 2$
$2 \times 2 = 4$
$2 \times 5 = 10$
$2 \times 3 = 6$
$2 \times 6 = 12$
$2 \times 4 = 8$

teddy bear I have a cuddly **teddy bear.** He naps with me.

telephone I call Grandpa on the **telephone.** I talk to him and he talks to me.

television I see moving pictures and hear sounds on a **television**—or TV.

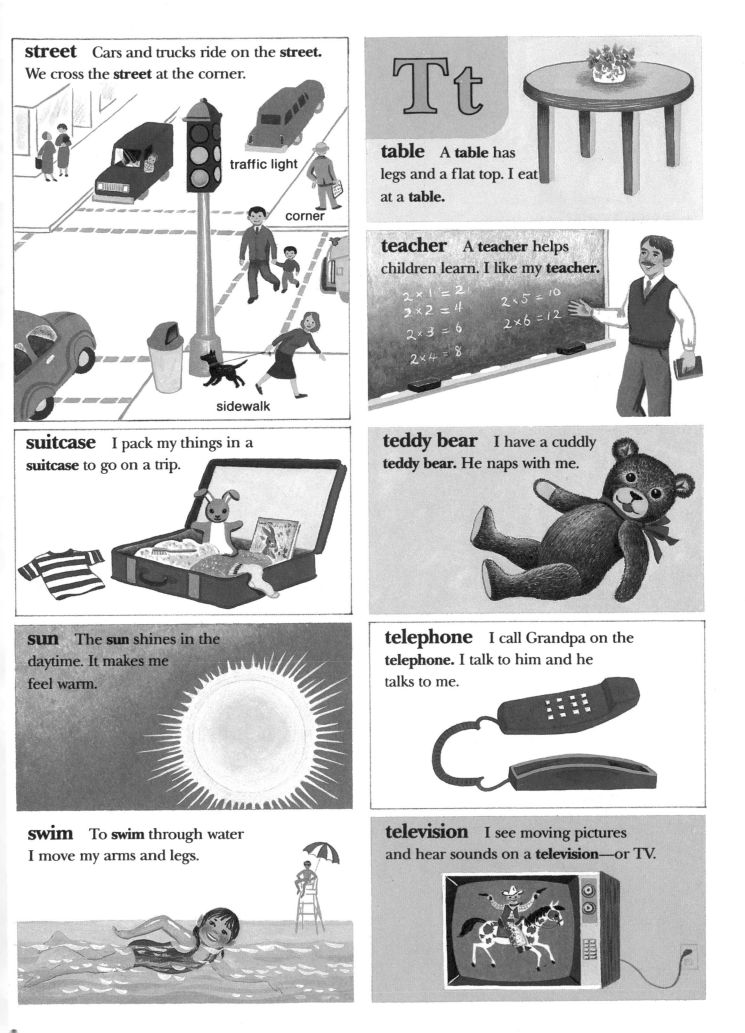

tent We sleep in a **tent** when we go camping.

thermometer Mommy takes my temperature with a **thermometer.**

tool A **tool** helps us do work. Daddy has many **tools.**

screwdriver

hammer

pliers

saw

wrench

drill

toothbrush I brush my teeth with a **toothbrush** and toothpaste.

toy A **toy** is something to play with.

top

blocks

marbles

horn

doll

action figure

train A **train** runs on a track. I listen for the **train** whistle.

tree A **tree** is a tall plant. It has a trunk, branches, and leaves.

truck A **truck** has a motor and sometimes many wheels. It can haul heavy things.

turkey A **turkey** is a big bird. It says "Gobble, gobble, gobble."

turtle A **turtle** has a hard shell. It moves very slowly.

vegetables **Vegetables** are good to eat. They keep my body healthy.

beans

peas

onion

potato

tomato

beet

radish

carrot

corn

lettuce

Uu

umbrella My **umbrella** keeps me dry in the rain.

violin A **violin** makes music when I pull a bow across its strings.

underwear I wear **underwear** under my other clothes.

Ww

wagon A **wagon** has four wheels and a handle. I pull my puppy in my **wagon.**

Vv

valentine I made a lacy **valentine**. It has a heart shape on it.

I LOVE YOU

walk To **walk** I move my feet. I **walk** down the steps.

water When it rains, **water** falls from the sky. We drink **water** from a glass.

whale A **whale** is a big animal that lives in the ocean.

whistle When I blow my **whistle,** it goes "Tweet."

woman A **woman** is a grown-up girl. My mother is a **woman.**

X x

X ray An **X ray** is a picture of the inside of my body.

xylophone A **xylophone** makes music when I strike the bars with wooden hammers.

Y y

yarn **Yarn** is heavy thread used to knit.

Z z

zipper A **zipper** holds clothes together. My jacket has a zipper.

zoo A **zoo** is a home for wild animals.

bear

seal

monkey

lion

giraffe

tiger

zebra

deer

snake

wolf